Pebble® Plus

Plant Life Cycles

The Life Cycle of a
Bean

by Linda Tagliaferro

Consulting Editor: Gail Saunders-Smith, PhD

Consultant: Judson R. Scott, Current President
American Society of Consulting Arborists

Capstone *press*

Mankato, Minnesota

Pebble Plus is published by Capstone Press,
151 Good Counsel Drive, P.O. Box 669, Mankato, Minnesota 56002.
www.capstonepress.com

1 2 3 4 5 6 12 11 10 09 08 07

Library of Congress Cataloging-in-Publication Data
Tagliaferro, Linda.
    The life cycle of a bean / by Linda Tagliaferro.
    p. cm. —(Pebble Plus. Plant life cycles)
    Summary: "Simple text and photographs present the life cycle of a bean plant from seed to adult"—Provided by publisher.
    Includes bibliographical references and index.
    ISBN-13: 978-0-7368-6710-8 (hardcover)
    ISBN-10: 0-7368-6710-4 (hardcover)
    1. Beans—Life cycles—Juvenile literature. I. Title. II. Series.
SB327.T34 2007
635'.65—dc22   2006020940

Editorial Credits
Sarah L. Schuette, editor; Bobbi J. Wyss, set designer; Jo Miller, photo researcher/photo editor

Photo Credits
Bill Johnson, 13
Bruce Coleman/Gary K. Smith, 5
Comstock Images, 21 (beans)
Corbis/photocuisine, 20 (seeds)
Dwight R. Kuhn, cover (seeds), 9, 19, 21 (flowers)
Grant Heilman Photography/Garry Runk, 20 (seedling); Jane Grushow, 15
Shutterstock/Graca Victoria, cover (soil); Marek Pawluczuk, cover (flowers); MBWTE Photos, cover (sprout)
SuperStock/age fotostock, 11
Unicorn Stock Photos/M. Siluk, 17; Tom Edwards, 7

Note to Parents and Teachers

The Plant Life Cycles set supports national science standards related to the life cycles of plants and animals. This book describes and illustrates the life cycle of a bean. The images support early readers in understanding the text. The repetition of words and phrases helps early readers learn new words. This book also introduces early readers to subject-specific vocabulary words, which are defined in the Glossary section. Early readers may need assistance to read some words and to use the Table of Contents, Glossary, Read More, Internet Sites, and Index sections of the book.

Table of Contents

Bean Seeds

How do beans grow?

Beans grow from seeds

that are planted in the soil.

Bean seeds are hard
on the outside.
Water and warmth
make the seeds sprout.

Growing

The young plant
grows roots, stems,
and leaves.

Some bean plants grow vines.

Other plants become bushes.

In summer, flowers grow
on the plants.
The bottoms of the flowers
turn into pods.

13

Beans!

Seeds form inside the pods.

The beans are ready

to pick in a few months.

We eat the whole bean pod.

Some beans are not picked
and the pods dry out.
In fall, the pods pop open
and seeds fall out.

17

Starting Over

Next spring, some of
the seeds will grow
into new bean plants.
The life cycle continues.

How Beans Grow

seeds

young plant

flower

pod

beans

Glossary

life cycle—the stages in the life of a plant that include growing, reproducing, and dying

pod—the casing around the seed of a bean plant

root—the part of a plant that grows mostly underground; food gathered by roots moves through stems to the rest of the plant.

seed—the part of a flowering plant that can grow into a new plant

soil—the dirt where plants grow; most plants get their food and water from the soil.

sprout—to grow, appear, or develop quickly

stem—the long main part of a plant that makes leaves

vine—a plant with a long stem that clings to the ground or another object as it grows

Read More

Bodach, Vijaya. *Seeds.* Plant Parts. Mankato, Minn.: Capstone Press, 2006.

Ganeri, Anita. *From Bean to Bean Plant.* How Living Things Grow. Chicago: Heinemann, 2006.

Hibbert, Clare. *The Life of a Bean.* Life Cycles. Chicago: Raintree, 2005.

Internet Sites

FactHound offers a safe, fun way to find Internet sites related to this book. All of the sites on FactHound have been researched by our staff.

Here's how:

1. Visit *www.facthound.com*

2. Choose your grade level.

3. Type in this book ID **0736867104** for age-appropriate sites. You may also browse subjects by clicking on letters, or by clicking on pictures and words.

4. Click on the **Fetch It** button.

FactHound will fetch the best sites for you!

Index

Word Count: 117
Grade: 1
Early-Intervention Level: 14